Paws in the Snow

A Lyon Lynx Clan Introduction

Nicole Dennis

Blurb:

When he turns 21, all Derick Atwater wants is to survive the traditional Party Row shots, pass his winter finals, and try not to fall deeper in lust for his mythology TA, Benoit Chevalier.

After receiving a strange journal with a mysterious phrase: *"Under the new moon, during deep winter, a cat will place his paws upon the snow for the first time"*, he starts to feel weird. His skin ripples. Muscles ache.

Though he would follow the dreamy TA anywhere, he isn't expecting to end up in the middle of a blizzard. Once the truth about his 'flu' is revealed, all Derick really wants now is to pass his finals, but first he needs to survive a very long night.

• • • •

Attention Readers: This book uses US English.

• • • •

FatCat Books Ink

Trademarks

The author acknowledges the trademarked status and owners of the following word marks used in this story:

Gatorade: *Stokely-Van Camp, Inc.*

Pepto: *The Procter & Gamble Company*

Zoom: *Zoom Video Communications, Inc.*

Pop-Tarts Cinnamon Roll: *Kellogg NA Company*

Canvas Learning Management Platform: *Instructure, Inc.*

The Clash of the Titans (2010 Film): *Warner Bros., Legendary Entertainment, Thunder Road Pictures*

The Clash of the Titans (1981 Film): *Charles H. Schneer Productions*

Jeep Compass Latitude 4x4: *FCA US LLC*

The first edition of *Paws in the Snow* was released with the limited-edition anthology: Virgin Shifters: Shifting for the First Time.

An extra note: We could be seeing more of Derick and Ben in future books – The Lyon Lynx Clan.

Chapter 1

Holy fuck, he was never ever going club-to-club shot drinking ever again. Not even if he could celebrate his twenty-first birthday all over again.

Groaning when his stomach rolled again, Derick Atwater wondered how long a hangover could last. His friends dragged him to all the clubs on Saturday night since he would get one free shot from every club when he revealed his birthday thanks to flashing his license to enter.

With every 21st celebration, there was a competition between everyone in their collection of dormitories to see how far the birthday kid could get along the street the university students nicknamed Party Row. The rules were simple. One shot per club. No puking. Once you puked, you were done. Your shots were tallied and added to the boards. The one with highest tally gets a prize at the end of the semester – fall and spring.

All twelve clubs. All twelve shots downed. No puking.

He could now claim the record. Alone.

Though, holy hell, his belly wanted to kill him now.

Since that crazy wacky night, he felt rotten. It was more than a simple nausea-filled stomach. Muscles cramped throughout his body. Headaches. Fatigue. Part of him wondered if it could be the flu, which would seriously suck to have during finals.

Another roll of his stomach made Derick groan again. He placed one hand on the sink and stared at the bathroom mirror.

"You will *not* puke your guts. Not now. Not here. Suck it back," he ordered. He pointed a finger at his reflection. "Last half hour of work. Get through one class. Then study and bed. That's it. You will get through this day."

Splashing cool water across his face, Derick cupped and let water slide across the back of his neck. Finishing up, he blotted off the droplets with a towel, washed his hands, and left the room. He adjusted the deep blue apron with the campus bookstore's logo stitched across the front while he returned to the floor.

Lucky for him that it wasn't a busy workday. Everyone was either in the library, computer labs, or various study groups to complete final papers and prepare for exams. He should be in the library with everyone else, but he needed to keep this job to subsidize what he received from the scholarships.

"Hey, Derick, go ahead and clock out," the store manager, Kenney, said. "We're not busy. You need the study time before your class."

"I need the hours for the work program—"

"I'll make sure you're covered," Kenney interrupted him. "Clock out. If this blizzard hits like they predict, we'll be closed for the rest of the week. The store will send out an email once the campus officials decide. Stay safe out there."

"Will do. Thanks, Kenney, appreciate it. Same goes for you." Derick went to the computer, opened the time clock system, logged in, and put in his hours and code.

Ken added his supervisor code, a reason, and extended Derick's shortened hours to the full shift. Then he saved and closed the program. "See ya later. Try to get sleep. You don't look like you're feeling yourself."

"Still feeling the effects of my twenty-first binge party."

"Shouldn't last that long. Was it your first time doing that?"

"Twelve shots in one night. Yeah. Never did that before. Never again."

"Right. Don't blame you. Keep up with the hydration. Perhaps grab a few Gatorades from the other side of the store before you head out. Wouldn't hurt to grab some Pepto to calm down the acids. Try to eat something more than that banana you grabbed for your break. You need something in your belly." Kenney waved.

"Will grab the Gatorade. And the Pepto. Good thinking. I have food back at my dorm."

"Been there. Done that. I know some of the tricks. Do you have a class tonight?"

"Yeah, last review class for my Classical Studies: Greek Mythology."

"Lots to review."

"Complete with the Greek alphabet and names. We cover all of the Greek gods, myths, and legends."

"Yikes. Take care."

"Appreciate it. Again." Derick untied and yanked off his apron. He picked up his reusable water bottle and wiggled it. Then he headed toward the back area for store employees.

There were three sections to the campus bookstore. The entire back was dedicated to all the textbooks, but it was empty this time of the semester. The front right was a regular bookstore that sold fiction, nonfiction, and magazines. The front left was a regular corner store with the university inspired clothes, accessories, and gifts, along with various supplies, snacks, and drinks. Students could gather a bit of everything and anything and the prices were reasonable for the tightest of budgets.

In the back, Derick went to the bank of lockers. He spun his lock and opened the door. Then he pulled out the backpack, scarf, and hat. He tucked the bottle in its holder. When he pulled out his phone to check his messages, he noticed his mom called. He slid the phone into a pocket. Then he tossed the apron into the locker, closed the door, and twisted the lock.

Dropping the backpack on the table, he wound the scarf his mother knitted around his neck. Then he tugged on his heavy winter coat. He shoved the knitted hat into a pocket and pulled one backpack strap over his shoulder.

Making his way back out to the store and beverage area, he selected four bottles of Gatorade, a box of Pepto chewables, and bags of different snacks. Though nauseous, his belly gave a rumble of hunger.

Remembering Kenney's words, he grabbed a few other easy food items to help pass the time if the blizzard hit hard. At least he could keep eating if he couldn't get to the cafeteria. That is if his belly calmed down enough to let him enjoy his food without worrying about how fast he could reach the toilet. After checking out, he tucked his purchases into the backpack and slung it over both shoulders. He zipped up the jacket, pulled on his hat and gloves, and ventured out into the cold. After pulling out his phone, he called his mom while he walked toward his dorm.

"Hey, honey, I forgot you had a morning shift at the store. Sorry about the missed calls. How are you feeling?" his mother, Samantha, said when she answered the phone.

"Hey, Mom. Remind me to never go crazy drinking again. Please?"

His mom laughed. "Oh, honey, you're supposed to do all that crazy stuff now while you're still young. No one drove? Right?"

"Nah, we walked everywhere since Party Row is a couple of blocks off campus. Then I face planted in my bed and didn't move for twelve hours. Don't worry about the job, I managed to get the day off so I could sleep."

His mom laughed again.

"Thanks for the sympathy, Mom. Really."

Samantha chuckled. "You did it to yourself, darling. Perhaps it was better you spent your twenty-first while at campus and not home with your boring mom."

"Hey, now, you're never boring. Not my wild mom."

"Wild mom? Please—"

"Two words. Edible. Brownies."

"Hey, we swore to never mention that again."

"Uh-huh. My wild mom."

She snorted in playfulness at his teasing. "Truth. How are you feeling?"

"A little off. Might have picked up a cold or something. Since my birthday, things are off with me." Since he was always truthful with his mom, Derick knew he could tell her everything going on with him. Well, except maybe sex. He kept away from that subject, though he did come out to her long after she knew he was gay. She helped him figure out whether he was aromantic or asexual. They couldn't figure it out which way he flowed since he never had a full relationship. Raised by a single mom, who held down at least two or three jobs throughout his childhood to give him a better one, he respected and adored her and wouldn't hurt her by lying or cheating on anything.

"Oh, baby, I'm so sorry. Can you get through finals?"

"I have no choice, but to push through. It's the majority of my grade in every class. I didn't pick up cold meds, but I did grab Gatorade and Pepto. I didn't want the cold meds to interfere with studying or nodding off during an exam. Yes, I have meds if I get a fever or something to control it."

"Or you can stop off at the campus health center and get checked out."

"Maybe. Hate going there."

"Part of the perks of being on campus."

"Yeah, true. If I can't get there then perhaps when I come home, I'll zonk out on the sofa or you can drag me to the doctor if I don't kick this bug."

"Speaking of Christmas vacation. There might be a change."

"Why? What's happening?"

"Did you get my birthday package?"

"Yeah, thanks for the new scarf, hat and gloves. I'm wearing them now."

"What about Phillippe's gift?"

"I left it on my desk."

"Did you open it, baby?"

"Not yet. I don't know how I feel about... getting to know him." Derick kicked at a snow-covered rock while he thought about the Canadian man his mom slept with during her extended trip to Canada for a college semester abroad. Derick ended up being her extra souvenir along with finishing her associate degree. It didn't matter to her family. While they congratulated her on the degree, they condemned her for the pregnancy. When she wouldn't follow their orders to terminate the pregnancy, they kicked her out. When he turned eighteen, instead of asking his mother again for his father's name and information, Derick did the Ancestry genetics test and put in paperwork to find his father. Within a couple of months, Jean Phillippe Lyon contacted them.

"Phillippe is a part of our life. He gave me the most precious thing in my life. You. Derick, I never regretted meeting him or keeping you. Ever. He invited us to Canada to spend the holidays with him and his family."

"But he's married. With a whole new family."

"Not quite."

"What?"

"He's divorced and has custody of his children, your half-siblings. His wife took off with some guy, who promised her a home in France."

"How—"

"We've kept in contact since he first called you. We Zoom a lot to talk and it's been wonderful. Phillippe is a good man, Derick, and our connection never disappeared. Even after all this time. Don't blame him for what happened. Please. I was the one who didn't have the courage to find and tell him that he was going to be a dad. We were both young, kind of naïve, and from diverse backgrounds. It was a chance meeting that ended up with something wonderful for me."

"Moo-ooom."

"I know, baby. Sorry," she said.

"I'm not blaming anyone. I wouldn't change our life for anything. Other than wishing your family didn't cut you off so you wouldn't have to work so hard. That's it."

"I never wanted to rely on my parents. For anything. They didn't want me to go anywhere for college, they wanted to make me marry one of my father's partners' sons and be a pleasant housewife, raise a passel of kids, and become the elegant arm candy at parties. I refused. I would have been miserable being forced into that position."

"What? You didn't—"

"I know. I'm not too proud of them. Or my life with them. You already thought the worst of them, so I couldn't tell you everything."

"Until now."

"Because I don't want you to lose this chance to have an extended family to love and welcome you."

"Why should I give Philippe a chance? He's not a part of us."

"I would like him to become a part of our little family. Please give him a chance to add something more to your life. Open his gift. Think about his offer for us to visit Canada and his family for the holidays. You'll have grandparents, aunts, uncles, cousins, and a pair of half-brothers and a half-sister. And a father who hopes to get to know his oldest son."

"Okay. I'll think about it."

"Promise?"

"Pinky promise." Derick held up his pinkie finger and wiggled it though his mother couldn't see it. Though he knew she was doing the same on her end.

"Good. I'll text you his information. If you want to reach out, you'll have the ability to do it. I know he'll want to speak with you."

"Okay."

"I know not to press. The choice will be yours. Though, I know Phillippe will want to see you."

"Mom."

"Sorry. Sorry. I'm pressing..."

"It's okay. Just weird to think about it."

"I know. You're so busy now with the finals. Try to take a nap before your class, baby. Oh, make sure you take care with that blizzard. I heard it might be a doozy."

"I'm heading to the dorm now. I'll turn on the TV and see what's happening. The campus might be closed depending on how terrible the storm can get. Don't know the timing for the finals and holidays."

"We'll figure it all out."

"Oh, almost forgot. Stephen requested a scarf and hat. If you have time. He's jealous of my set. Same with a bunch of other guys on the hall. They're all impressed I have a mom that knits and makes things."

"Of course, baby, you know I love knitting while watching my evening shows. What colors?"

"The university's gold, black, and green. I'll give it to him after Christmas, if you finish, otherwise send it on over to me. It'll get colder here."

"I have a bunch of skeins in those colors. Perhaps I'll make a full collection of them if I have time and you can pass them out."

"You're awesome, Mom!"

"Back 'atcha! Love you, baby."

"Love you, Mom! Kiss!"

Derick hung up when he reached the dorm's double doors. He loved staying at this dorm since it was close to his classes and the bookstore. Even the rooms were a generous size for him and his roommate, Stephen Davidson, an engineer major. He tugged out his thin wallet from an outer pocket and pressed his student ID against the access panel. The doors buzzed and opened. He opened the door and slid inside the welcoming warmth of the building.

Within minutes, after dealing with all the call outs about his big Saturday night and record-breaking shots, Derick managed to get on the elevator up to his floor. He flipped around the wallet to use the key on the other end to open his door. Stephen was at the library for a marathon study session.

Derick dropped the backpack on his bed, peeled out of the winter clothes, and removed the polo shirt. He tugged on a soft old concert tee and his university sweatshirt over it for warmth. Then he turned on the

TV to listen to the weather while he unpacked his purchases from the backpack and tucked them away in their places. He managed to eat a pack of room-temp Pop-Tarts Cinnamon Roll since he had nothing but a banana and a candy bar. Then he crunched on a couple of Peptos and cracked open a Gatorade bottle to sip while he sat to watch the weather.

After the quick 'dinner', he stared at the wrapped package sitting on his desk. He pulled it closer and removed the envelope. Another quick tear and he read the written message from Phillippe Lyon. It was heartfelt with hope for a meeting. Then Phillippe mentioned it was a tradition to gift every Lyon scion a special journal for their 21st birthday. Even though they didn't know each other, Phillippe considered him part of the Lyon family and continued the tradition.

Derick ripped open the package to reveal a gorgeous leather-bound journal. He opened it to find Phillippe added a message on the first page:

For my son, Derick, on his 21st birthday.
A traditional gift for a son of the Lyon clan along with a family quote:
"Under the new moon, during deep winter, a cat will place his paws upon the snow for the first time."
Please contact me soon should you need any help or answers.
I'll be here for you from this day forward.
With a newfound love.
Your father, Jean Phillippe Lyon

There was a beautiful ink drawing of a large fluffy cat with dramatic pointed ears and stubby tail moving through a snowy forest background.

"What the hell does all that mean? Cats? Paws? Snow?"

For now, not sure what to think about it, Derick set the journal aside. Leaving the television on low, he set an alarm on his phone and dropped back on his bed. Within moments, he fell fast asleep for a much-needed nap.

Chapter 2

Waking up from the nap, Derick still didn't feel like himself. No matter how awful he felt, it was too close to finals. He couldn't miss his Greek Mythology night class. It happened to be one of his favorite classes. Especially since he would see the TA who taught for the professor. Early on during the semester, something came up in Professor Chaney's schedule and he passed the class on to his TA, Benoit Chevalier. There was something about the quiet TA with his black-rimmed glasses and long black hair with silvery strands that flowed around a lean face with his elegant French-Canadian accent and old-fashioned manners. Then there was the fact he needed to turn in the paper that counted for forty percent of his final grade.

At the thought of the paper, Derick picked up the blue folder that held the printed version of his paper. He flipped through it one more time for another proofing run. Like hell would he let a stupid comma or screwed-up verb mess with his grade.

Satisfied with the paper, he carefully tucked it into the presentation folder, attached the USB drive that he used for the class, and slid it into his backpack. Then he added the book and binder filled with his notes and folder of information. He grabbed his water bottle, emptied out the old water, and topped it off with fresh. Then he stuck it back in its pocket. Not sure why, but he added his father's journal. Might as well put it to use and he wanted to check out that drawing again. He slid in the protective case that held his netbook and cords. After a quick check to make sure that was everything, he zipped up the blue backpack before he could second guess himself. Finishing up, he tugged on his knit hat, wound the scarf around his neck, and slid back into his coat against the incoming blizzard.

Great damn timing, Mother Nature.

Grabbing his backpack, phone, and wallet, he turned off the television, walked out of the room, locked up, and stepped into the hallway. Using the whiteboard attached to their door, he jotted a note for Stephen. Then he headed down the hall to the elevator.

Zipping up and pulling on his gloves, Derick tugged the hat further down to cover his ears before he stepped outside. Bracing himself against the cold, he stepped outside and shivered at the wind seeping down to his bones. This was going to be one cold walk. He plodded his way across one central court covered in snow, a series of buildings, and reached the building he sought out. Entering with a couple of other students, he shook off the cold that managed to penetrate the layers.

"Holy crap! Feels like my balls shriveled," one student muttered.

Derick snorted. "Feel the same, man. Feel the same."

"Where you get all the woolen gear?"

"Package from Mom. She's a knitter."

"Can I get a set? I'll pay," the student asked with a wide grin.

"By the time she's finished with a set, winter will be over. She's a slow knitter." Derick lied with ease since he didn't know the guy. Plus, his mom would be knitting for most of his dorm friends.

"Damn. Gotta check my family and their lady friends."

"Finished your paper?"

"Last night. You?"

"Friday. Before I got dragged through twelve clubs and bars for my birthday," Derick admitted while they walked down the hallway to the small classroom. He bit his inner lip to hold back a moan when a series of painful spasms hit his muscles.

What the hell is happening to me?

"Are you the guy who drank all twelve shots without hurling?"

"Shit. How the hell—"

"Man, it's known across campus. In the right spots, especially on Frat Row. I'm sure some of the houses want to get you to rush for them." The student slapped a hand against Derick's back. "Way to hit the mark."

"*Oof.*" Derick grimaced at the hit that set off more spasms. "Yeah, thanks. Not really interested in a fraternity. Just had the right group of friends to drag me along Party Row." He rolled his shoulder after he turned the corner.

The student laughed while following him, still yakked about the great Saturday night bar crawl.

Quieting his grumbles, ready to kill his friends for gossiping, Derick entered the classroom. He glanced at the amphitheater classroom and regretted the stairs. With a grimace, he climbed the stairs, but didn't go to his regular spot. His body wouldn't let him move too far or too fast. Instead, he selected an aisle chair away from the frozen ball guy. Stripping off the outerwear, he tucked the scarf, hat, and gloves back in the pockets. He draped the jacket over a nearby chair. Then he dropped into the chair and released a long sigh.

"Ow. Shit. Damn. Why?" He snagged his water bottle and drank multiple gulps. He flipped open the desk next to him and set his bottle there to keep it within reach. Then he pulled out the journal. Since he had it, he figured he might as well use it to finish up the semester. He ran out of space in his other one with all the end of the semester readings, papers, exams, and notes.

Within moments, he jotted down updated notes, times, and plans in a makeshift bullet journal pattern. Then he added new tasks to remember. Though, he added a note about the weather and possible time issues. Then he flipped back to the front to read the note and odd quote while looking at the drawing of a fluffy large cat.

Tapping the end of his pen against the journal, he closed and tucked it back. He replaced it with the class binder, book, and presentation folder. As per the code, he pulled out his paper and handwrote the moral and ethics clause on the last page and signed it. Other students around him did the same things.

After tucking the paper back into the folder, Derick rocked a little and rose from his seat. When he rose, his muscles cramped. Hard.

"Ow. Ow. Shit. Damn. Ow," he muttered.

Wishing it were simple as cracking his back or doing something to release the pain, Derick rolled his neck and held back everything. Still, he forced himself to walk down the steps along with other students. He stepped in line and placed his folder on top of the stack left on the desk.

"Good luck with the paper," the annoying student said.

Derick managed a grin, rolled his eyes after he turned, and returned to his seat. Once again, he slid back. His body felt like he traveled a hundred miles instead of a couple of stairs.

A rush of sweat beaded down his back.

"Again? What the hell is happening?"

Once again, he rolled his head around to stretch his neck muscles. Reaching out, he picked up the bottle and took small sips of water from the bottle.

"Just get through the class and you can sleep."

Chapter 3

When the door opened, the doctoral student and teaching assistant Benoit Chevalier entered the classroom.

"Good evening, class," Chevalier called out. His tone rolled with a French accent that softened his words. He pulled off his heavy winter coat and draped it over a chair. "Welcome to our last face-to-face class. It has been my pleasure to teach all of you this semester about the classical myths and legends of Greece. I hope everyone learned a little bit more than they expected."

A different sensation raced through Derick when the older man appeared. Something drew him to the tall, black-haired TA. More than anything like a friendship.

A deep attraction.

He didn't want it to end because the semester was over. Not that he would be leaving the classical studies. It made up the most of his classes, along with the art department.

"Any updates on the weather, sir?" someone called out.

"There is an update, but I will get to that in a few moments. Promise," Chevalier said while he tapped the presentation folders together. "Thank you for these papers. It'll keep me busy during the storm for my review and Professor Chaney's grading to determine the final marks."

The students laughed.

"As usual, the grades will be posted on our class website. I'll return the USB drives to your on-campus post office boxes. Don't forget to pick them up before you leave campus if you want to reuse them next semester." He wrapped a rubber-band around the folders and tucked them into his messenger bag. "There will be a change in our class time due to the incoming blizzard. The entire campus is closing at nine pm."

He checked his watch. "That gives us an hour and a half tonight. Unless a weather update beeps on my cell phone."

"What else do you know?"

"As you know, a light snow is falling now, but this will become worse. Campus officials want all students and faculty in their dorms or homes before the worse hits and roads become too slick for travel. Campus will be closed until the blizzard passes, except for the cafeteria and library. All other stores and restaurants are closed. All activities and on-campus jobs will be canceled until further notice."

"Exams?"

"Still unknown at this time. As of this update, they will move all exams to the Canvas online system across the board. This doesn't change our class, since, like the mid-term, your final exam on Canvas will open for two days. You must complete and submit the exam within those two days. Be sure you can access the Canvas program from your dormitories or off-campus housing in case you need to contact the support offices before they close or get inundated with issues. If this blizzard worsens or becomes extended, then the exam days might be changed. Along with Winter Break."

Most students groaned.

"I know. I know. It sucks. Make sure all of you keep an eye on texts, website, campus TV channel, and emails for updates and changes." Chevalier lifted his gaze and looked over the room. "Any questions?"

No one said anything.

"Okay. Let's jump into the final review for your exam. Since our review class is cut short, I will hold multiple review sessions on our class message board for any questions, concerns, and assistance." Chevalier called up a screen onto the board that held the main points. "Your final exam will cover all of the chapters after the mid-term. This encompasses everything regarding the heroic myths and motifs. Like the mid-term, you need to remember the Greek spelling of the names. Please review the pamphlet I passed out with the pictures of the statues and paintings.

Some will be in the exam and you'll need to name the hero and legend. You should recognize the Greek spellings and give the English version of them. Please review all of that on your own. We'll cover the last topics here in class. Anything else can be managed online."

"What about that movie we watched? *The Clash of the Titans*?"

"It might pop up as a bonus question."

"Which version?"

"Both. The directors did a fairly decent job in presenting the Greek legends."

There was some grumbling at his answer.

Setting up his attack for the review, Chevalier jumped into the review. He moved to another screen that highlighted certain areas. "Chapter Twenty-one. Perseus and the Legends of Argos."

Derick jotted notes to point out what he needed to review on his own for the upcoming exam. There were a few things he could refresh to do better. He made notes to fill out new flash cards with the Greek names and re-watch of the movies.

Whenever he tried to concentrate and take notes, Derick felt something roll hard through his head and belly. Then it caused a series of cold sweats racing down his spine. Pressing a hand to his belly, he held back a painful moan of agony.

"Not again. Not now. Come on, go away," he muttered.

Bugs creeped and crawled underneath his skin. Every single bone and joint ached. He twisted his head back and forth and heard multiple vertebrae cracked and popped. It didn't help.

Could this be the start of the flu? A truly nasty case of it. He never felt this bad.

What could possibly be worse than this feeling?

Before he could stop, things listed in his mind. From illnesses to simple flunking his exams if he couldn't get over whatever was happening.

If he didn't maintain his grade point average every semester, he would lose his scholarships and ability to pay for school. Without that money, he couldn't remain here. The only option would be to sign up for expensive student loans with their crazy interest rates that would kick in the moment he walked away with a degree, but not job. Trying to avoid all that expense, he tried to stay away from the loans. Nor would he dare to ask his mom to co-sign a parent loan. She worked hard enough during his childhood to provide the best for him. He would figure out his own way to make his dream of being a museum curator and art restoration expert come true.

He needed to deal with this stupid flu. Concentrate on his studying. Get through the exams. Then he could collapse during the break.

Stick to the plan, Atwater.

"Mr. Atwater, a simple question. After advice from Hermes and Athena, where did Perseus go?"

Derick felt his mind scramble to come up with the answer. He knew the answer had something to do with three old ladies who shared an eye. But for anything in his bones, he couldn't remember the Greek name that Chevalier would want. He stared at the notes on the screen and his notebook.

The effort set off another round of painful cramps and sweats.

"Mr. Atwater?" The handsome TA climbed the stairs to check in on him. "Do you remember the answer? They appear in multiple myths."

"To locate the Graeae, the three daughters of Phorcys, sisters of the Gorgons, and old women since birth. They can see all, but will only part with their information under duress," Derick answered.

"Excellent." Chevalier touched his fingers to Derick's shoulders and bent down. He lowered his voice to keep things private. "Are you okay? You seem a bit off this evening. Other than the distraction of the blizzard."

"I'm okay. Did a little too much this weekend. It was my birthday."

"Can you continue?"

"Yes. Yes. I'm good."

Chevalier shook his head after he checked him over. "I don't think that is the correct answer. Stick around a few extra minutes after class. We'll have a chat."

"The blizzard—"

"Just a few minutes since the blizzard is causing havoc."

"Okay. Sure."

"Good. Now..." Chevalier walked down the stairs. "Did Perseus get his answer?" He pointed to another student to continue the review.

"Crap. Crap. Crap," Derick muttered after Chevalier moved out of hearing range. Then he groaned when a burning sensation attacked his eyes. "Ow..."

The TA glanced over his shoulder and looked at him. He tilted his head and a strange expression covered his face.

The burning sensation disappeared.

Derick rubbed his eyes and hoped that wouldn't happen again. When he opened his eyes, Chevalier moved further down.

Chevalier pointed to another student to check in and see if they understood the myth of Perseus. After condensing the rest of Perseus's adventures, he moved on to 'Heroic Motifs'.

Throughout the review, Chevalier condensed the material due to the reduced time they had together. In a way, he kept the review manageable for everyone. He notated certain sections they should concentrate on studying during the downtime before their exam time opened on the Canvas system.

At certain intervals, Chevalier checked the weather system for updates, then proceeded to the next chapter.

Throughout the next half hour, Derick dealt with multiple waves of pain and sweats. He managed to take a few more sips of water, but it didn't help. Then he swore to himself that he could feel something strange stretch and roll deep inside of him. It was the craziest sensation.

He dug his nails into his palm to hold back an curses and shouts of pain while his body continued to betray him.

This was the strangest onset of flu he ever went through.

Another weather alert dinged loud on Chevalier's computer.

"Hold that thought." Chevalier moved his fingers across the laptop to read the latest update.

"What does it say, Professor?"

"Not good news for our review, I'm afraid. All classes are to end immediately," Chevalier said.

Several students groaned at the announcement.

"I apologize for the change. According to the university's president, all students are to head straight for their dorm or off-campus housing. No sidetracks or deviation. The weather situation is becoming quite dangerous. Please, everyone be extremely careful outside. We will continue our review online. Please check your emails for my notice when I open the message boards for any assistance."

"How are we going to get together?"

"It'll be done during multiple times on different boards. I don't have a specific time spot set up for the review board." Chevalier held up his hands when some students tried to complain. "I apologize for cutting our reviews short for the exam, but from what I can tell, you all know and understand the material."

A few students agreed.

"Remember to keep your attention on your emails and texts, the university's website, their on-campus TV channel, and other places for all updates. Don't forget the local weather for the blizzard. Be smart. Don't rush out to the bars or parties, nothing will be open. Okay? Let me repeat. The bars will be closed like the rest of the town," Chevalier reminded them.

Most of the students laughed.

Derick could only groan at the memory of his last visit to those damn bars. It put him in his horrible situation.

"Good luck to everyone with this blizzard. Safe travels to all. Good luck with your exams." Chevalier waved. "Shut it down. Get home safe."

Chapter 4

Exhausted from the waves of pain, Derick slowly packed up his backpack and tucked the bottle in the outer pocket. Zipping it up, he slung one strap over his shoulder and grabbed his coat. Carefully, he walked down the steps.

Though other students called out to him, he ignored them. Just not feeling strong enough to answer.

He leaned against the front row desks. Dropping his coat on one desk, he rubbed his fingers over his head and rubbed his neck.

Dark speckles filled his vision. Then the strange burning sensation returned to his eyes.

"Do you know what is happening to you, *mon chaton*?" Chevalier asked in his soft French-Canadian accent.

Lifting his head, Derick tried to blink through the speckle spots and burning. "Happening? Flu. Got flu."

Chevalier shook his head. "Not the flu. Something special. Something that I don't think you ever learned about, but now I can see it inside you. I can help you, but you must trust me. You will need to listen to me, follow me, and I'll get you through what is happening." He touched his fingers against Derick's cheek. "Can you do that for me, *mon chaton*?"

"Will I feel better?"

"Oh, *oui*, better and stronger. That I can promise."

His knees buckled when another wave of pain and cramps roared through his body. He groaned and collapsed.

"Oh, *mon chaton*, we're running out of time," Chevalier said when he caught him. He held Derick tight against his frame.

"Feel horrible... Help me, Professor—"

"Ben. Call me Ben."

"Scared. Feel horrible." Derick rested his head on Chevalier—Ben's shoulder. He breathed in the soft fragrance of Ben's cologne. Just the touch and smell of him comforted whatever happened deep inside him. "Don't leave me."

"Never, *mon chaton.*"

"Help me?"

"Of course. I should have known what you were earlier. You look so much like him. I thought I was looking at his younger mirror when we first met all those months ago. Your name shook me a little," Chevalier said.

"Him?"

"My childhood friend, Jean Phillippe."

Derick leaned back and looked at the older man.

"Do you know the name?"

"Jean Phillippe Lyon?"

Chevalier smiled. "Lee-own," he pronounced the name with a French sound. "Do you know him? You resemble him like a mirror image, except your face is a touch softer which must be from your mother."

"My biological father."

"Then he knows—"

Derick shook his head. "Never really spoke to him. Just a card now and then."

"I don't—"

Derick moaned in pain and shuddered.

"Not the time for such a deep discussion. We must get going." Chevalier helped him back to his feet. Then, like a child, he assisted Derick with his coat. He quickly got into his outer gear.

Then keeping an arm around Derick's waist, Chevalier assisted Derick out of the classroom.

The blizzard roared and blustered around them. Wind whipped around their bodies, blew snow all over, and sent waves of heavy snow across everything.

Their footsteps were soon hidden under a fresh layer while they made their way across campus to the closest parking lot.

Ben unlocked a deep blue colored Jeep Compass Latitude 4x4. First, he helped Derick into the passenger seat and tucked his bag on the floor. Then he tossed his bag in the back seat and grabbed a snow and ice scraper. He extended the handle and used it to remove the layer of snow and light ice from the exterior. Once it was fairly cleaned, he climbed into the seat, turned on the engine, and turned up the heat.

Another wave of pain rolled through Derick. "Hurts."

"I know. The first time hurts the worse. The heat will help until we get there."

"What is happening to me?"

"Your body is preparing for the change. Did you turn twenty-one?"

"Saturday. Preparing for the change? What change?"

"A transformation. In a special and unique way. Just hold on. A little difficult to drive, but we're not going far," Ben said. He brushed his fingers through Derick's sweat-saturated curls. "You're not alone, *mon chaton*. Since you are Jean Phillippe's son, I will take care of you and help you with the transformation."

Turning in the seat to lean closer to Ben's warmth and scent, Derick closed his eyes against the waves of pain. Then he opened them a bit and watched the snowy world flash by the Jeep's windows.

Maneuvering through the blizzard, Ben drove carefully off campus and went a few more streets away. He turned into a gated community and waited for the gate to open. Then he drove through the smaller neighborhoods filled with townhomes and villas. Winding around to the last neighborhood, they reached a collection of five-plex buildings placed at the very back. Then he turned into the driveway at the end villa. He clicked a button and parked inside the garage. He turned off the car and moved around to help Derick.

"Welcome to my home," Ben said while he gathered their bags and helped Derick out of the seat.

"Nice. Now... what?" Derick's voice broke on another vicious wave of pain. "Ow. Ow. Feels like bugs under skin." He rubbed his hands over his arms. The friction made the sensation even worse.

"Going to drop off our things. Then I'm going to tell you how things are going to proceed and it's going to sound and act a little weird. But this will help you," Ben said.

After Ben opened the inner door, he helped Derick through the foyer hallway. One side was a door to a study and a bathroom on the opposite side.

Though barely aware of his surroundings, Derick wanted to check out Ben's chosen home. After passing a bedroom, the hall opened to a larger floor plan to encompass the kitchen, eating area, and living room on the right side. To the left was another doorway.

"That's my bedroom suite," Ben said. He dropped their bags on the sofa when they made it to the living room.

Derick wavered on his feet. His eyes burned. Something sharp moved through his body. He thought his bones might snap and break.

Pulling off his coat, Ben moved to stand in front of Derick. He placed his hands carefully on either side of Derick's face to gain his attention.

"Hurt..."

"Ssh. Listen to my voice. Focus upon it," Ben said.

Derick listened.

"I need you to strip off all your clothes."

"What?"

"Please, let me reassure you that what I'm asking will help. I promise. There is nothing sexual about what I'm requesting."

Trusting Ben's words, Derick managed to undo his heavy winter coat.

Ben stepped away and disappeared into his bedroom. He returned with a robe draped over his arm.

When Derick's hands shook too much, Ben assisted him in removing the heavy boots, socks, and the rest of his clothes. Then Ben wrapped him in the robe.

"Follow me."

Not sure what was happening, Derick managed to follow Ben to the patio door. They stepped outside on the patio. Then Ben opened the outer door.

They went all the way outside.

The blizzard blustered and blew around them. The biting cold wind whipped around them.

For some reason, this time, the bitter cold didn't bother Derick. Not even his bare feet that sunk deep into the cold. He stared down at his feet. "I'm not cold."

"No, your body is becoming accustomed to what is happening to you," Ben said. "Follow me."

Ben continued to draw him further away from the villa and deeper into the forest. "This is a national forest that connects to my neighborhood. It's why there's no fence or wall, it wasn't allowed due to one rule or another. We'll have more privacy out here."

"Privacy for what? What is happening?"

"You inherited the ability to shift and transform your human form into an animal. If my assumption is correct, you will become a lynx."

"My mom can't do that."

"This genetic ability came from your father, Jean Phillipe. His family are well known shifters in Canada. Along with my family. They are very strong shifters. A wonderful clan."

Derick looked away at the thought about his Canadian father, Phillipe. A cat? Was this what the odd quote in the journal meant?

Not pushing Derick to explain in his current position, Ben smiled and touched Derick's face with his fingers. "Though I thought I recognized your father in your appearance, there was a distinct change in your scent tonight. Then your beautiful peridot eyes flashed to a hazel when I asked you that question. Perhaps your eyes burned."

"They did. My eye color changed."

"Yes. Eye color is one of the first to change. Though, I thought you might have inherited the genetics because of your pale white-blond hair and soft curls. It's a common trait in multiple clans. Your father has the same hair and eye color.

"There isn't much time. Your transformation will happen soon. It isn't pleasant the first time while your bones, muscles, and nerves all reshape and connect. It hurts like hell. Though it will last only a few minutes, it will feel forever. I'll go through the basics of shape-shifting. I wish we had more time, but this all we've got to work with at this moment."

"Shape-shift? Like a werewolf in movies and books?"

"Like that, yes, but since you're Jean Phillippe's son, you'll become a lynx. Along with wolves, we're the next more prevalent species of shifters on this continent. Now, I'll talk you through what is happening. Listen and focus on my voice. I'll get you through the transformation," Ben said.

Something harsh and devastating rolled through Derick. Deep cramps rippled underneath his skin and muscle. It felt like his skin would split open. Every bone and joint hurt. Heat rose through him.

Wrapping his arms around his belly when it felt like something kicked him in his guts, Derick called out in pain while he bent over.

"It's okay. Your body is adjusting. It's learning about the new genetics and what needs to happen. Let the pain wash over you, Derick. Accept the power and the transformation. Accept and welcome your cat," Ben said. "It'll hurt like hell this first time, but after your body learns what to do, the shift will get easier. Each new moon, your transformation will happen smoother and faster."

After multiple waves of this type of pain and rippling sensations, Derick let Ben remove the thin robe and tossed it over a nearby branch.

Pain overwhelmed every system within his body.

Derick couldn't speak. Only sounds and cries of pain escaped.

Then he collapsed into the soft mounds of snow. He dug his fingers deeper into the snow, but the freezing cold didn't assuage the fiery pain.

His bones cracked and broke. Tendons stretched and snapped. Nerve endings fired out of control, overwhelming the pain sensations within his brain. His skin rippled from head to toe.

His entire body twisted and jerked. It transformed and remade itself into another formation. His bones reconnected and grew. Powerful muscles attached along with tendons.

His cries of pain turned into a feline's yowl.

Then he collapsed onto his side.

His first transformation complete.

Chapter 5

Derick flopped into the building snow on his side. He shivered from the overwhelming experience. He kept his eyes closed while he tried to remember how to breathe.

"There you go. Wonderfully done. Rest now. Let your body acclimate to the changes. Such a pretty *mon chaton*," Ben said while he remained close. He continued with his soft encouragements to soothe his scattered mind.

Then he felt Ben's fingers stroke his fur.

Fur!

Derick opened his eyes to a different experience, vision, and world. Everything was different. The colors weren't distinct and sharp, but his senses of hearing and scent were heightened. He swore he could hear each snowflake land. Then he rolled up, lifted his head, and looked down.

Paws!

Instead of his hands, he discovered the large pair of fluffy paws. Did that mean—? He flexed them. Massive claws flexed out from the tips.

Fluffy murder mittens!

He flexed each paw and watch the claws appear and disappear inside the tips. Then he turned one paw to study the dark pads surrounded by long white fur. Thick fluffy fur covered his entire body along with another set of paws. With a touch of concentration, he flexed the back paws to figure out how they worked, along with the joints that bent in a different fashion.

A stubby tail flicked from his butt. A stubby tail.

That's it?

"Oh, come on, that's it for a tail?" Instead of words leaving his mouth, all that happened were meows and yowls. Grumbling, Derick sat up on his rump. More cat sounds left him. Then he lifted a paw and licked the side of it.

When that happened, he stopped and stared at his paw and back at Ben.

Ben laughed and stroke one of Derick's ears. "That's instinct for you, taking over our minds. It's a way for your cat to cope with the stress and discomfort from the first transformation. Even shifters have this natural-born instinct within their cats."

Derick twisted and flicked his stubby, black-tipped tail.

"You're a Canadian Lynx. Because we often live in areas that have deep layers of snow for long periods of time, the lynx developed with elongated limbs and short tails to help them maneuver through the habitats."

Derick sat again. He wanted to flick his tail and chase it like he saw kittens do.

"Oh, don't be such a grump about the tail. Get up on your paws, move around, and try a little pouncing on the snowflakes. You need to become accustomed to your new form and how to use it."

Derick stayed put. Other than lift a paw and lick it again. He glared at that paw.

Ick! Hairballs!

"Come on. On your paws, *mon chaton*." Ben encouraged with multiple scratches and pets around Derick's thick facial fluff. "Oh, such a big, sweet baby. Here you go..." He teased while he played his fingers along the large ears with their long black tufts. Then he dragged his fingers along the fluffy tufts along Derick's jawline and down to the fluffy chest.

Derick purred under all this attention. Then he chuffed at all the odd sounds. He glared at Ben, who chuckled.

"Get used to it. You might have some human thought, but it's still a cat's body. Cats can't use human words. Now stop being lazy and get up."

Umm. Cat! Supposed to be lazy. Catnap?

"Up. Gotta get moving."

Flicking his ears at Ben's insistence on moving, Derick rolled to his paws. Then he planted all four paws and rose on the elongated legs. He pulled back and stretched out his shoulders and legs. Then he reversed his position to stretch his haunches. He even lifted and stretched each leg and paw to figure out how to move everything. Comfortable on his paws, he moved around in the deep snow. He discovered he could spread his toes out wide to act like snowshoes and not sink as deep in the soft snow. It felt different to move the four paws in the deep snow.

Derick pranced away, snuffled around in the snow, and checked out all the different scents. He sneezed multiple times when his sensitive nose got a bit too much.

Then he returned to Ben's side. He rubbed his head and body against Ben's legs. Then he could smell the lynx within Ben. He chuffed at him.

"I'm not shifting this time. We're too out in the open in this forest," Ben said.

Derick meow-yowled to encourage him.

"No, not this time. Go on and run around. I'll keep watch," Ben said while he scratched behind Derick's ears.

Derick flicked his ears.

"Go on. Have fun. Learn how to be a cat, a lynx in the wild. Enjoy this first shift," Ben said.

With Ben's encouragement, Derick danced away through the snow. He raced out through the natural forest, enjoyed all the scents, sounds, and sensations of flying across the snow on steady paws.

Hours later, when he was about ready to turn and head back to Ben, Derick stopped and dropped into a crouch. His tail stood out and flicked. His ears moved.

There. A soft crunching in the snow. Something light and small.

Derick sniffed the wind.

Rabbit!

Carefully moving closer, Derick wiggled his backside and leapt high. He pounced down on the small, thin rabbit and smacked it with his massive paws. When he heard the crunch, he whined at what he did.

Death! I killed a rabbit. Oh no!

Not sure what to do, Derick snatched up the rabbit and pranced back toward Ben and the villa. He realized he could track his way by following Ben's scent on the wind. When he appeared out of the tree line, he spotted Ben leaning against an old oak for some shade and cover from the snow and wind.

"What do you have there?" Ben called out.

Derick went to him and dropped the dead rabbit at Ben's feet. He plopped on his rump and meowed.

"Did you kill it?"

Derick chuffed. Then mewed.

"Impressive. Not many first-time kits can catch such a stealthy prey. Your father will be proud," Ben said. He crouched in front of Derick and his prey.

Derick mewed. He killed. With his paw, he nudged the dead bunny.

"It's okay. You did what you needed. Instinct. Do you want to eat it?"

Derick pulled back and bared his teeth. *Why would I want to eat Bunny Foo Foo? Ick... Oh, wait, cat.*

"They usually are on the menu for wild lynxes. Plus, we often catch and enjoy them during the clan gatherings."

Derick shook his fluffy head. He lifted a paw and licked off the blood and fur. Then he grimaced at the taste. *Yuck!*

"It's an acquired taste. Like deer. A venison, deep in the natural woods, type of flavor filled with trees and grass."

Derick shook his fluffy head.

"Okay. Okay. I know there is a trio of young foxes out here. They'll find your dinner and enjoy it in this cold." Ben picked up the rabbit by its ears and moved back into the tree line to place the rabbit in a safer spot for the young hunters. Then he returned to where Derick waited for hm. "Time to get you back to the villa. The blizzard is getting worse, even for us. These are dangerous temperatures. Stay in your cat form." He snagged the robe and led Derick back through the forest, across the strip of horticulture land between the wild and human dwellings. When they reached the back porch, he opened the door. "Shake off your fur and paws."

Derick started the shake from his ears, through his head, his neck, chest, and along the rest of his body. Even down to his stubby, black-tipped tail. He lifted and shook each paw. Then he stepped through the doorway after each long shake to remove the snow clumps.

"That's the way. You're learning a bit at a time," Ben said with another scratch to Derick's ear.

After opening the slider door, Ben returned to lock the screen door.

Derick went all the way inside and circled around by the fire.

Ben followed him, went to the trunk that was a coffee table, and opened it to pull out a large fluffy blanket. He spread it out as a nest of sorts. He pointed to it.

"Rest for a bit. Keep in your cat form."

Derick padded across the wooden floor and sniffed along the blanket. His lips pulled back when he caught the scent. Then he recognized it belonged to Ben.

"Yes, this is often my bed when I need to a turn as a lynx. Go on," Ben said. He moved to the fireplace and placed a proper stack of starters, kindling, and logs. Then he pulled down a box and slid out one long match. He struck it with a single pull and placed the flickering flame against the starters and kindling. When the flames caught in multiple places, he used the poker to build up the fire.

With a yawn, Derick circled the blanket nest a couple of times and curled up on the fluffy softness. He rested his head upon his paws and watched the flames.

"Shifting, especially the first time, takes a lot of calories and energy. The first thing as a young kit, you must either learn to eat what you catch as a lynx or have a supply of protein and calories waiting. Never ever go without either option. Understand?"

Derick stared at him and blinked his eyes.

"I have something in the fridge." Ben gathered up Derick's clothes and placed them on a chair along with the discarded robe. He went to the kitchen.

Derick watched him walk away. He twitched his whiskers and wanted to lick the rest of his body. Somehow, he resisted the urge.

Within a few minutes, Ben returned and dropped a plate filled with pieces of cold chicken and chunks of red meat.

Derick sniffed, ate all the pieces, and licked a bowl of water empty. Instinct drove him to clean his fur. He couldn't resist the urge again. Yawning, he licked his lips.

"Go on. Take a nap. You're safe with me." Ben stroke Derick's head between his ears. "It'll help with the later transformation back to your human self."

With another yawn, Derick rested his head back on his paws. Then he slid deep into a nap in front of the fireplace.

Hours later, feeling refreshed, Derick opened his eyes. When he looked down, he realized he remained in his lynx form.

Okay, not a dream, not some crazy shit. I really changed into a lynx. A walking, breathing, purring lynx. That wants to keep licking its fur.

"Hello. Welcome back. Yes, you're still a lynx," Ben said.

Looking around, Derick stared at his paws. Then he looked back up at Ben.

Ben's hair was damp from a recent shower. He dressed in older sweatpants, T-shirt, and a heavy cable-knit sweater. He wore thick socks on his feet. Moving his body, Ben dropped into a sitting position. "Ready to get back to being human?"

Derick chuffed. *Duh. Need some questions answered.*

"I'll talk you back through a reversal of the transformation. This first time, it's going to be painful again as your body readjusts and acclimates.

Whatever happens, you keep moving through the transformation. Don't stop." Ben stroke his head again. "Understand?"

Derick meowed.

In the same fashion, Ben spoke in a soft tone to help bring Derick from his lynx form back to his human form.

The horrible pain returned throughout his body. His bones cracked and reshaped along with the joints, tendons, and skin. His skin crawled and itched while his fur retreated. Then something strange happened in his back while his tail disappeared.

Derick coughed a few times. He spat out wads of fur.

Damn lick bath.

"Yes, that can happen sometime after an extended shift. Especially with kits."

Naked, sweaty, back in human form, Derick rested upon his side on the blanket. His muscles trembled from the effort to return to human. He tried to remember how to breathe.

"Hang in there. The sensations will pass in a few minutes," Ben said. He draped an incredibly soft blanket that he pulled from the chest over Derick's body.

Derick rubbed his cheek against the blanket. "Soft."

"Your skin will be extremely sensitive until the new moon passes."

"Why?"

"It has something to do with the first change. Our scientists and historians are still figuring out things. It happens during the first six moons of a new kit. After that, the sensation dissipates for the rest of their life."

"Good to know." Derick rolled his head back and forth. Then he cleared his throat a few times. It was dry and hoarse, like he sucked down a mouth full of fur.

Ben pushed himself up and disappeared from Derick's sight. He returned with a glass full of water. "Drink up. It'll help with the dry throat."

Derick swallowed until the glass was empty. "Thanks. How long?"

"Were you out?"

Derick nodded.

"About six hours. It's around three."

"In the morning?"

Ben nodded.

"Why are you wide awake?"

"All cats are on the new moon. We get extra energy, except for new kits. The first shifts exhaust them."

"Feel wrung out."

"That's normal." Ben sat on the trunk's edge. "How about a shower?"

"Yeah, need that."

"Good. Let me help you up and I'll show you around," Ben said. He assisted Derick to his feet. Then he wrapped the soft blanket around Derick's nude body. "After you shower, I'm make us something to eat and answer the immediate questions. By then it will be time for a good nap. Later, you can connect to whom you need."

"Good plan."

"One step at a time. You're taking things remarkably well," Ben said while he led Derick through the villa to the master suite and into the adjoining bathroom. He opened the door and twisted the showerhead to a rainfall patter. Then he turned on the water to a lukewarm temperature. While he did this, he explained everything to Derick.

"Would being hysterical change anything?"

"No."

"There you go. Always felt something was a bit different about me. Other than my sexuality," Derick said.

"Sexuality?"

"Mom thinks I'm in the demisexual range. Though, I'm also gay, just not into..."

"Jumping every guy you meet at a bar or in a class within thirty seconds of meeting them," Ben said.

"Right. What about lynxes?"

"Most are bisexual, but there are ranges for everyone." Ben slipped back to this bedroom and returned with a stack of clothes. "Here's something for you to wear. Oh, and use these towels." He pulled out two soft towels and washcloths. "They shouldn't aggravate your skin."

Derick maneuvered the blanket to free a hand and placed it on Ben's forearm. "Thank you. For everything."

Ben smiled. He placed his hand against Derick's cheek. "It was my pleasure to help you through your first transformation. Your full initiation ceremony and acceptance to the clan will happen when you meet your father. Until then, it'll be you and me."

Derick grimaced about the idea.

"Something else to talk about. Enjoy your shower."

Derick looked around the comfortable space and back to Ben, who moved to the door.

"I promise. You'll remain safe here. Lynxes only get frisky during and after transformations about five years into shifting or they found their mates. Until then, things are quiet. Even if they weren't, I wouldn't even dream of touching you. Though, you are a gorgeous young man." With those words, Ben winked at him and slipped out the door to leave Derick alone.

Chapter 6

After a gentle shower, Derick used the soft towel to pat dry his sensitive skin. He winced at the flickers, but the sensation became less with the passing moments. Squeezing out most of the water from his hair, he ran his fingers through the curls to let them drip dry. Then he yanked open the plastic covering on the new boxers and tugged on a pair. He carefully wiggled into the sweatpants and T-shirt. Sitting down, he pulled on the soft, fluffy socks. Thanks to his mother's teachings, he hung up the wet towels before he left the bathroom.

Along the way, he felt a whole lot clearer in his head. All the pain and hangover-like sensations dissipated since his shift.

Holy hell! I shifted, completely totally transformed, into a cat! A lynx.

Pausing in the hall, Derick placed a hand on the nearest wall. He leaned toward it and pulled his breath in and out. Now he needed to figure out what next to do. Then he remembered how he had someone special to guide him. Someone he wanted to get to know more. Beyond being such a wonderful teacher.

"Suck it up. Time to figure out what is happening. Get a move on."

With the pep talk, Derick pushed away from the wall. He shoved fingers through his damp hair. Making his way back down the hallway, he smelled the comforting scents of grilled cheese sandwiches and tomato soup.

"That smells so good," he said when he entered the open floorplan of the kitchen and living room.

"A little better offering than the potential little Bunny Foo Foo meal you contemplated," Ben said with a chuckle after giving the sandwich a final flip to check for coloring.

"Ugh. I can't believe I almost ate a bunny. Fur and all," Derick said. He held his hand to his belly. "That wouldn't have been a pleasant sensation coming out."

"Your body will adjust. Actually, I'm impressed such a newbie could catch and kill a bunny in the middle of a blizzard."

Derick leaned against the counter. This time, he voiced aloud what happened to him. He hoped it would sink into his brain. "I transformed into a lynx."

"Yes. Yes, you did," Ben said. "Again. I need to point it out. I'm amazed that you're taking what happened in such stride without freaking out."

"Oh, I'm freaking out. Trust me. Inside, my mind is going a million miles a minute." Derick tapped his fingers on the counter. "Why me?"

"You don't remember much from before the shift?"

Derick shook his head. "Not really."

"Do you remember me mentioning Jean Phillippe?"

"You knew him. And I look like him."

"Yes, almost his exact mirror. Because of that resemblance, you inherited the genetics that allow you to transform your physical shape." Ben looked over at him. "Have you ever heard the phrase: *'Under the new moon, during deep winter, a cat will place his paws upon the snow for the first time.'*"

Derick's jaw dropped.

"I take it that you have. Somewhere."

Derick turned to look around. Finding his backpack, he walked to it and opened the zipper. Then he pulled out the journal. Hearing his phone buzzing in a pocket, he tugged that out too. He carried everything back to the kitchen area. Then he opened the journal to the first page and spun it to show Ben.

Ben wiped off his fingers after transferring the second sandwich to a plate. Leaning over, he studied the page. "This is Jean Phillipe trying to reach out to you. To explain what might happen to you. It's not always a definite possibility, especially with a parent who isn't from a shifter clan. Now, you don't carry his name. Correct?"

"It's complicated."

"I thought it might be from your earlier answers. You can tell me whatever you desire, but I promise not to push further."

Derick played his fingers along the counter's edge.

"Sit down. Eat." Ben set a plate down with the sliced sandwich and generous bowl of soup on the counter. He added a napkin, spoon, and glass of water. "Your body needs the water and calories."

Derick hitched up to sit on the counter stool. He drank half the glass.

Remaining in place, Ben carried a stool around so he could face Derick while they talked and ate. "Okay. How about you try to explain your complicated situation with Jean Phillippe? We can't go anywhere for a while and I know you're curious and filled with questions."

In between bites and sips of soup, Derick talked about his mom met Phillipe and how he came around. "Our name came from my mom's Aunt Helen and her husband, Peter, who took her in when Mom escaped her family. I learned her parents wanted her to get rid of me by adoption or abortion and marry a business partner's son or something. It was horrible. Anyway, she escaped them and went to Aunt Helen and Uncle Peter, the black sheep of the family, and they took us into their family. Mom changed her name to Atwater and gave it to me since she didn't tell Phillippe."

"But you never met him?"

Derick shook his head. "No, I never met or really spoken to him."

"How did you learn about him?"

"When I turned eighteen, I ordered one of those genetic tests, spit in a tube, and sent it off. Then when I got the results back, I showed it to my mom and asked her about my father. I said it was time I knew the truth."

"What did you know before then?"

"Only what I told you. For school, I lied and said he was a soldier who died. The timing was around all those wars against terrorism. It got me through school without a lot of questions. Any heritage or family tree lines were based on my Aunt Helen and Uncle Peter, not my mom and me." Derick thought about it. "Hey. What happened if those tests figured out my shifter genetics?"

"You tested before your twenty-first birthday. The genetics begin the change during your twentieth year. Until then, they remain silent, perhaps show as abnormal, but nothing unusual to be further examined."

"Oh, that's a good thing. Wouldn't want to reveal the big secret."

"It's not a full secret, just kept private." Ben ate half of the sandwich. "What happened after your mom gave you the information?"

"I reached out to him and explained about my mom, me, and our connection. Just got a few letters and cards since my eighteenth birthday. Then I got the journal as a gift for my twenty-first. I opened it before I went to your class."

"Which happened on Saturday?"

"Yup."

"Which are the triggers for a first shift. A kit will turn twenty-one, there will be a new moon, and a deep cold front or blizzard will happen. All three things are key to allow a kit to shift for the first time."

"Kit?"

"A new shifter. That's what the clans call their young ones."

"Do you come from one of these clans?"

"My clan lives outside of Montreal. Your father's clan is outside of Toronto. The main hunting grounds are north, closer to the southern end of Hudson Bay. It's also where all the clans get together every three years to introduce new kits, younger shifters meet each other, and territorial disputes or issues are discussed and organized."

"That's how you got to know my father."

"Yes, we became good friends over the years."

"Am I old enough to be your son?"

Ben smiled and studied him. "How old do you think I am?"

"Mid-thirties. You're working on your doctorate."

"My sixth doctorate."

Derick's jaw dropped.

"I'm 257 years old at my last birthday. Your father is 260 years old."

"What?"

"We stop aging in our thirties, and age one year every thirty or so years. Our scientists are trying to figure out the reasoning behind our slow aging."

"My mom—" Derick stared down at his dish.

"Will age and pass. That's the most complicated issue with being a shifter. Those we love, who do not carry the gene or shift, will leave us."

"That sucks."

"In time, it's something you will learn to adjust to the reality."

"Don't know if I ever would. What else do you want to know?"

"It might be helpful for us to contact Jean Phillippe to explain what happened. Usually, if we were back in Canada, there would be a full ceremony, a run, and other things to celebrate a kit's first shift. Not all children inherit the full genetic code to shift. Some will carry the genes, but not shift. With half of your code coming from your father and a non-shifter mother, I'm surprised at your strength and skill for a kit. Sometimes, a kit needs to shift multiple times the first night or couple of nights to control their lynx. I can sense that your cat is settled and happy."

Derick pressed his hand to his chest. He felt his internal lynx curl deep inside him, somewhere deep, flicking the long fluffy tail, and purring. "Purring. I feel... purring."

"A strange sensation. I know."

"That's... crazy."

"Your lynx is now a part of your life."

Derick munched on the last of the delicious grilled cheese sandwich. His phone buzzed again. "Sorry, do you mind?" He motioned toward the phone.

"Go ahead."

Flipping the phone over, Derick swiped the code in to unlock it. He grimaced at all the messages from Stephen. He hit the button to call him back and set it on speaker mode. "Do you know what time it is?"

"Screw the time. Where the hell are you? Do you know there's a massive blizzard out there?" Stephen demanded.

"Hello, Stephen. Yes, Dad, I'm fine. No bones broken."

"Ha. Ha. Ha. Funny guy. Really, man, you scared the shit outta me. I got kicked out of the library and heard the night classes got canceled. I've been calling and texting you since that time. You never showed up back in the room."

"Sorry. Sorry."

"Did your illness get worse?"

Derick looked up at Ben, who nodded. "Umm. Yeah. I passed out in class. Since the health center closed, my TA, Professor Chevalier, gave me a lift to the ER. A bad sinus infection and cold. They gave me fluids, antibiotics, but they wouldn't release me unless someone could keep an eye on me. Someone a little more reliable than another stressed college student. The professor brought me back to his place. I just got back up and on solid ground. It's really late for both of us to be up," Derick said.

"Hello, Stephen, this is Benoit Chevalier, Derick's TA for Greek Mythology. He's fine. Just needs a couple days of rest. He'll spend the blizzard with me, and I'll bring him back to campus. We're not far. Just off campus by a couple of streets. The neighborhood of villas," Ben said.

"Hey, Professor," Stephen said. "Yeah, I know the place. I'm up because I'm finishing up my studies before the exams start up. Everything is being moved online, same schedule. Only laboratory exams will be in class and those might be late."

"Neither one of us has one of those exams," Derick said.

"Yeah, which means everything we have is online. My first one is on Thursday."

"Don't study too late. Make sure to get some rest and food."

"Yes. Yes, I know."

"Don't worry about Derick, but I would listen to his advice," Ben said.

"I hear both of you. Okay, take good care of my roommate. I don't wanna break in another one," Stephen said.

Derick snorted.

"Thanks for checking in on him. I apologize for not contacting you, but Derick's phone was locked, and I didn't have the code," Ben said.

"That's okay. Happy to know he's still alive. Lemme know if you need anything, Derick," Stephen said.

"Will do. Thanks." Derick ended the call.

"Nice of him to be worried," Ben said.

"Yeah, he's a good guy. We've been together since Freshman year. Though, he's one of the instigators who dragged me to all twelve bars on Party Row on Saturday for my free shots. So, I'm not sure I like him all too much."

"How did that go?"

"I tried to do it the smart way. Made sure to eat something greasy at the first stop, kept a water bottle and drank it every two stops, and made sure to only order one type of liquor. Tequila with a lime and salt. Licked the salt, took the shot of tequila, and finished with a lime wedge. All twelve bars. No puking."

"That would be your natural metabolism, an extra benefit of becoming a lynx shifter. We're able to contend with a little more abuse of liquor, calories, and physical hits. Not that I recommend doing it every day."

"Is that why I survived all twelve shots without puking? Just a minor hangover. Other than feeling horrible."

"Yes. The feeling horrible was your body's adjustment and changes to accept the genetic alterations and upcoming transformation. It was preparing you for the pain of the first shift." Ben refilled their water glasses. "I wish I recognized the signs earlier and I would have alerted you to the changes and what was to come."

"I should have spoken to my father."

"That might have helped too."

"Thank you for what you did. Getting me out of the classroom and taking me through the shift."

"Again, I'm amazed at your resilience and acceptance of what is happening to you," Ben said with a smile. "A remarkable kit. Not many accept or believe in these changes so readily. Especially if they lived as an outsider, like you."

"You got me through it."

"I'm happy to help you."

Derick yawned after finishing the second glass of water.

"The exhaustion hit."

"It did. Sorry," Derick said on the edge of another yawn.

Ben glanced toward the nearest window. "Dawn is approaching. Even if I can't see the glimmers of it through the heavy clouds, I can feel it after all these years."

Derick looked at the couch, but back to Ben. "Is it weird that I don't want to sleep alone?"

"No, not at all. After all the changes, you need the comfort of another being. Someone who understands."

"Could I —"

"I promised nothing sexual would happen. Yes, you can sleep in my bed with me." Ben collected their glasses and plates, rinsed them, and placed them in the dishwasher. He did the same with the two pans. Then he moved around to check the windows, locks, and tampered down the fire to let it burn to ashes.

When he finished securing the house, Ben clicked off the lights and took Derick's hand. He collected their phones in one hand.

Derick shuffled after Ben to the master bedroom. After Ben pulled back the covers, Derick curled up on one side. He watched Ben plug in both phones to charge.

Sitting on the edge, Ben fiddled with his phone for a few moments. He disappeared into the bathroom for a few minutes. Then he returned and settled in the bed next to him. Pulling up the covers, he tucked them in.

Derick adjusted until he was closer, but sleep dragged him down before anything else could happen.

Chapter 7

Waking up in slow stages, Derick came back into awareness. There was a heavy weight around his lower waist and hips, but it was comfortable and steady. The sheets were softer than his usual set. He snuggled against something warm and a bit harder than his favorite pillow.

A steady rhythmic thumping against his ear. The scent familiar to him.

Blinking to clear the sleep from his eyes, he noticed how weak light poured into the room through the curtains. A chill rolled down along his backside while his front was toasty warm. Everything was eerily quiet.

Outside the room, a powerful wind blew around. Branches tapped along the windows and building's exterior.

Returning his attention back to the room, he lifted his head and semi-recognized a faded T-shirt that covered a muscular chest. The chest rose and fell with each deep steady breath. He twisted a bit to stare at the sleeping face of Benoit Chevalier. His TA. His savior from the pain. A lynx shifter.

At some point in the night, he must have turned and snuggled against Ben's body. His body unconsciously searching for warmth and comfort after the recent traumatic events.

When he pulled his hand back across Ben's belly to try and slide away, Ben stopped him. His larger hand covered Derick's hand. Ben gently squeezed Derick's fingers.

When he looked up again, he watched Ben wake up to the same awareness of their snuggled position.

Ben blinked a couple times. Then a sleepy smile curled his lips. He yawned off to the side and stretched a little underneath Derick's weight. "Morning. Or afternoon."

"Morning," Derick said.

"How are you feeling? Any cramps? Creepy crawling bugs under the skin sensation?"

Derick assessed his body from head to toes. "Skin is a bit sensitive, but nothing else. I feel much better."

"That's good. You might not need another shift. Keep an eye on those feelings. If they come back, we might have to go back out in the woods for another shift and run."

"Is that a good thing? Not needing another shift."

"It means you're a strong kit."

"Guess that's good to know." Derick nuzzled his cheek against Ben's shirt and chest. He paused after realizing what he was doing. Like a feline marked their human guardian, he wanted to mark his scent on Ben. "Umm. Sorry about—"

"The snuggling? Don't be. I enjoy the closeness. Same with the marking. It's all instinct." Ben repositioned his hand until his fingers could play with Derick's pale curls.

"Me too," Derick said. He twisted until he stretched along the bed. He moved his legs to work out some kinks in his knees. Then he folded both hands under his chin to rest between Ben's chest and his chin. With that bit of a boost, he could take in the rather glorious view of the older man.

Ben continued to play with Derick's curls, wrapped one ringlet around his finger a few times, but he didn't pull or yank.

Derick kept still under the gentle touch. He felt the connection grow between him and Ben. He didn't want anything to drag him from this position. Then he thought about something horrible and grumbled.

"What is it?"

"Umm. This..." Derick wiggled his chin on his hand. "Between us. It isn't going to come back at you. Right?"

"Back at me? My TA and doctoral position."

"Yeah. Is my being here going to hurt you?"

"No, my personal life is my own. While I do grade papers and tests for your class, the professor has the final say on all the grades."

"Oh, good. Cause if I take more of your classes, which I might, I don't wanna stay away from you outside of them."

Ben grinned and flicked one of Derick's curls. "I feel the same way."

"Good." With that settled in his mind, Derick sighed and settled back into the comfortable viewing position.

"What time is it?"

"Don't know. Didn't get that far in waking up. Enjoying the view." Derick wiggled his eyebrows in a playful fashion. He felt his dick perk up and take notice, but kept the sensation tampered down. *One step at a time.*

With a soft chuff of laughter, Ben released his fingers from Derick's curls. "Come on. Let me move."

Sighing, Derick curled and sat up. He adjusted the covers to let them fall around his hips.

Free of Derick's weight, Ben twisted and reached out one arm to pat the nightstand. When he couldn't find them, he grumbled under his breath. Lifting off the pillow, he focused off to the side. "There it is." He pulled up one of their phones and hit a button. "Almost eleven in the morning. Not too bad. Oh—"

"What?"

"I think we lost power. The charging icon is off. Battery is full."

Derick adjusted further way to give Ben room to sit up at the announcement. Not what he wanted to here, but something they should have expected with the strength and duration of the blizzard. He reached across Ben's body and scooped up his phone. When he got yanked back, he mumbled and popped off the charging cord. Free of the connection to the wall, he pressed in his code to open his screen. "Full power here too. Yay for that." Then he settled in to check his messages. A couple from the school, his mom, and Stephen. Nothing major. Then he checked the news. "Uh-oh."

"What did you find?" Ben leaned over to study Derick's screen.

"Power outages reported all over the area from the blizzard. The weather news team estimates we have another six hours of this to go through so crews can't get out to assess or repair. The government requests everyone remain at home. Don't go out. Roads blocked by down lines, trees, and snow and ice," he said.

"Guess you're staying with me a little longer."

Derick smiled. "I don't mind that at all."

"Me neither. I enjoy having your company in my home," Ben said. "And my bed." He added the last part with a wink. Then he slid off the bed and disappeared into his closet. He returned with two heavy sweaters and tossed one to Derick.

"I thought we're supposed to run warmer. Least that's what all the stories say."

"We may be shifters and run a little warmer than normal humans, but to combat this kind of cold uses more calories. Easier to add another layer and conserve your energy for other things. It's all about balance."

"Yet another thing for me to figure out as I navigate through this new path of my life."

"Yes. Need another pair of socks or slippers?"

Tugging on the sweater over the outfit Ben gave him yesterday, Derick wiggled his toes. "No. I'm good for now."

"Let's get that fireplace going to warm things up. It puts out a decent amount of heat, but we'll shut the doors to the other rooms to keep it to the main rooms. Then I'll find my camp cookstove and gear to make some coffee and breakfast."

"Why do you have camping gear?"

"When I go back to Canada for gatherings or I want to take a longer trip into the woods around a new moon. I may be a lynx, but I still prefer my human comforts outside of the fur. A warm meal that's not covered in fur and bones. A hot cup of coffee in the mornings. A bit of extra light. Even able to blow up a mattress. It's the little stuff."

Derick chuckled and followed Ben through the house. "I appreciate all the little stuff too."

"Good to know. Perhaps we'll go camping in January. It'll be the beginning of a new semester, not as much pressure."

"I like that idea."

Ben glanced over his shoulder. "Good." He went to crouch next to the hearth. Then he scooped out the cold ashes.

"Put me to work and tell me what to do."

"We'll need some more logs and kindling. There's a pile of both stacked in the garage. There's a flashlight on the wall between the laundry and garage and right next to the door," Ben said. He held out the sling log carrier. "Use this to carry everything. Makes it easier."

"Got it," Derick said, grabbed the handles, and went off down the main hall. When he reached the entrance to the garage, he found the flashlight where Ben said. He clicked it on and entered the garage. He used its light to search the freezing garage. "Dang, it's cold in here." He shivered while his feet curled. Staying focus on his job, he located the pile of logs and kindling. Then he stacked six logs in the bag and topped it off with the kindling. He carried everything back, made sure to place the flashlight back in its wall holder, and shut the door behind him. Then he continued down the smaller hall, closed the other door to conserve the heat, and returned to the main rooms. He set the carrier next to Ben. "Is this good?"

"That should last for a while. Do you know how to build one?"

"A fire? Nope."

"Come and learn. A good lesson to know," Ben said.

"Can't stop being a teacher."

"Nope. Longer you delay, the colder it gets."

With a chuckle, Derick sat next to Ben.

Within a few minutes, to Derick's pleasure and pride, the fireplace had a good-size fire that put some heat back into the room. Ben deemed it excellent work for a first timer.

Needing another trip to the garage, Ben got Derick to follow him. They brought two plastic tubs back inside the house. Ben placed them along the hallway. Then he returned to the garage and carried three red containers of gasoline and set them by the door to the patio. He opened the tubs and pulled out different items.

"Do we need all of it?"

"Not right now. Take these lanterns and place them in different areas. Keep to the kitchen and great room." Ben reconnected the batteries in the large ones. Then he popped in fresh batteries in the smaller ones.

"You got it." Derick picked up the multiple types of lanterns and placed them around the countertops and living room tables. He turned on the largest ones to illuminate the area. "What about candles?"

"We might add some later, but these will do for now." Ben carried the camping stove and small coffeemaker into the kitchen.

Then Ben bundled up to set up an inverter generator on the patio. He placed a prepared piece of board with a small hole cut out to thread the cords through to spread them out. After pouring in the gas, he cranked it up and closed the door. With Derick's help, they plugged in the fridge to protect the food. Then Ben connected a smaller coffeemaker and got it going brewing a fresh pot.

"Should I tape down the cords in a couple of places?" Derick asked while he toed one of the thick orange cords.

"Sure. There's a roll of masking tape in that drawer next to you," Ben said.

"Okay." Derick found the tape and made quick work of taping down different spots of the largest orange cords. "How's that?"

"Better. Should be a bit safer."

"Happy to help out," Derick said and returned the tape to the drawer.

With quick movements, Ben pulled out what he needed from the fridge and pantry. He turned to check with Derick. "How about omelets?"

"I can go with those."

"Quick and easy." Ben whipped up the eggs in a bowl.

"Can I help?"

"Dice up the veggies. Bacon is already crumbled. Cheese is shredded." After locating a board and knife, Ben placed both in front of Derick. Then he connected the camping stove to a portable propane tank to heat up a pan.

Derick sat and diced up the scallions, roasted red pepper, and leftover mushrooms into neat piles on the board. He carried it over to help Ben place a collection of each in the middle of the prepared egg. Then he picked up a plate to allow Ben to flip and slide the omelet out. He remained next to Ben, while he started the second omelet.

"I got the rest," Ben said. He set the used board and knife in the sink once he cleared it of the veggie piles.

"You are handy to have around in a natural disaster," Derick said while he carried over his plate to place it on the counter. Then he returned to pour himself a mug of brewed coffee and doctored it how he liked. "How do you like your coffee?"

"Double cream. No sugar."

"Got it." Derick fixed up Ben's coffee. He carried both mugs to the spots they chose last night. This time he sat down on the far side. Once Ben turned off the stove, removed the propane tank connection to render it safe, and carried his plate over, Derick savored his cup of coffee. He didn't eat until Ben sat with him.

"How am I handy? Is it because I know what I'm doing?"

"And you have all this cool gear."

"Only took a couple hundred years of practice."

"Still can't wrap my mid around that. Wonder if my mom knows about Phillippe's age."

"Have they been talking?"

Derick nodded. "She told me they spoke a lot on the phone and over the computer on face-to-face calls. I think she's still in love with him, but now that all this happen—"

"If Jean Phillippe loves her, he will tell her everything about him and you."

"Though I should talk to him first."

"Might be helpful. We can generate enough of a signal on my phone to connect the computer and contact him over the computer. Best do it face-to-face instead of a phone."

"You wouldn't mind."

"I wouldn't have mentioned it if I did." Ben smiled and slid the forkful into his mouth.

When his phone rang, Derick glanced at it and slid his thumb across the screen to answer the call. Then hit the speaker button. "Morning, Stephen."

"What's happening by you? Is your power out?"

"Yup. But I got a cup of coffee, an omelet, and a roaring fire."

"Bastard."

Derick laughed. "What about you?"

"Cold cereal. Everyone is in the common room on each level to stay warm. We're all in layers and blankets. Everything is out. We're in the Dark Ages. Studying is the main thing, but some are playing board games and cards. Gotta eat the stuff in the fridge and freezers. All of us are moaning for caffeine. Can't get to the cafeterias, everything is shut off."

"Poor Stephen."

"Shad up."

Derick laughed again at his roommate. "Guess I'm staying put. Got it good here."

"Bastard." Stephen cut off the call before Derick could laugh or respond.

"Guess that's how things are going at the dorms." Derick slid his phone back. Then he finished the rest of the omelet.

"Unless your entire floor troop through the snow and show up on my doorstop," Ben said

Derick laughed. "I wouldn't put it past them when it comes to caffeine cravings." He carried his plate to the kitchen. Then he topped off his mug with more coffee and a touch of cream. Locating a sponge and soap, he checked for the water supply. He let out a little cheer when it ran clear, perhaps it came from a well or something. Then he got busy washing the different items Ben left in the sink.

"You don't have to do that."

"You cooked. I clean. This time I'm at least semi-mobile and alert to do this," Derick said.

Ben lowered his plate into the sink along with the silverware. He poured the last of the coffee into his mug. "Want me to start another pot?"

"Of coffee? Sure. Could use some while I study. Oh, do you have index cards?"

"For your vocabulary?"

"Yeah."

"Sure. I'll get them from my office. Anything else?"

"That's it. I should get some studying done. Then, perhaps, we could call Phillippe."

Without saying a word, Ben pressed his hand to Derick's lower back to support his decision. Then he grabbed a lantern and went off to the front room that he turned into his office.

Finishing the simple task of washing dishes, Derick unplugged certain things to stop excessive use of the generator. He carried the full carafe and a potholder to the table and placed it down. Since Ben left the creamer out from breakfast, he carried the box and sugar over to make it easier to grab. Then he finished with a pair of large lanterns to provide the light.

Not liking the silence other than the crackling fire, Derick dug through the two bins until he found a small radio. He popped in the batteries and placed it on a counter. Pulling out the antenna, he turned it on and found a local radio station that played music and kept them updated on the weather.

Satisfied, Derick grabbed his backpack and carried it over to the table and chose a spot. He pulled out his book, the pamphlet Ben created from all the gathered information about paintings and statues of the mythologies, and his binder. At the bottom, he found his collection of index cards from previous study sessions.

Humming along to the music, he flipped through the cards to pull out what he needed for the final exam and set aside others. He made additional notes on different cards. Pausing in his work, he topped off his coffee mug and added a touch of creamer.

"Here you go. Along with different colored pens and markers. Brought my own work," Ben said when he returned. He dropped of the items and chose a seat. He placed his own bag on the chair.

"Do you mind the music?"

"Nope. Was going to suggest it myself," Ben said while he pulled out the stack of paperwork to grade.

With a smile over his coffee cup, Derick got down to the business of studying and creating the index cards for his vocabulary and a straightforward way to break down the legends. He lost himself in the multiple legends and lives of the ancient Greeks.

Chapter 8

Hours later, complete with a break of simple sandwiches and chips, Derick leaned back in his chair. He stretched his arms, shoulders, and neck. "Ugh. Nothing else will sink into my brain."

Ben chuckled. "That's how studying can get. Doesn't change no matter how old or how many times you take classes."

"Are you a perpetual student?"

"There's always something new to learn."

"But you're away from your family and clan."

"Most of the times, yes, but I follow something that I love to do. Since I have multiple siblings mated and bearing children, I'm not needed to continue the line. It's an important part of the clan, but there are reasons we can slip away from those responsibilities."

"What if we know we're mostly gay and thinking about..."

"It's no longer frowned upon for those kits who lean gay or lesbian. There are other ways to conceive. More modern views are slipping into the clans and adjusting the culture and rules." Ben folded his hands across the table and leaned forward. "Clan life isn't perfect. Like everything else within this crazy world, there is good and bad. While most of us may shift into lynxes, it doesn't take away the certain details in humanity. For some nasty ones, the change intensifies them. Most clans challenge these lynxes, stamp them down, and control them. Some are..." Ben shrugged.

"Removed permanently?"

"If that's the only way to protect the clan and society, yes. There is a prison system for shifters, and we do send prisoners there, but for some of the worst cases—" Ben shrugged again. "They don't give us a choice. Case in point, a pair of brothers hunted humans. They kidnapped, tortured, raped, and hunted their human prey. It took several years for our law enforcement to locate and capture the brothers. They placed them in the prison, but they managed to escape. They hunted again. At that point, at an unprecedented multi-clan council meeting, they brought down a judgment of death upon the brothers."

"Holy shit," Derick said.

"It was a truly horrendous case and outcome. That is the worse things can get within the clans, but the benefits and life of a lynx far outweigh the danger." Ben tilted his head. "Did I scare you off?"

Derick shook his head. "Nope. Filled in some answers."

"Good. How about we contact Jean Phillippe?"

"Yeah."

With a nod, Ben collected his laptop, power cord, and cell phone. He popped one earbud into his ear and handed the other to Derick for his ear. Then he carried everything to the sitting area by the fireplace. "Over here will be better. I'll call him and give him a bit of a surprise. Stay over there until I call you over," he said. He plugged the charger into the generator's power. After turning on the laptop, he created a hot spot on his phone and connected a video call.

"Benoit, hello, what an unexpected pleasure to see you calling. I didn't expect this," a warm voice said over the speakers and the earbuds. The accent was like Ben's voice.

"Jean Phillippe, how wonderful to see you. I hope you are well," Ben said.

"I am. Getting things ready for the holiday season and big gatherings. How goes the teaching?"

"Goes well. Almost time for finals. I'll be home with the clan for a couple of weeks during the break."

"Hope to see you when you return to Canada," Jean Phillippe said.

"There is a reason I called. I apologize, but things will be kept short. We're under a blizzard and power outage. I'm connecting this call on my phone's hotspot and it's not going to last long," Ben said.

"We?"

"I have a surprise for you. One of my students became a member of your clan last night with his first shift to a lynx. He's a wonderful, strong young kit. Someone you'll be proud to know. He's here with me," Ben said.

"Who is it?"

Ben motioned to Derick.

Derick moved closer and sat next to Ben on the loveseat. He waved and smiled at the screen. He couldn't believe how the man looked exactly like him. "It's me. Derick."

"Derick..." Jean Phillippe's jaw dropped after he whispered Derick's name. "Son... Oh... I..."

"Surprise," Ben said. "I recognized your face in him. Then his eyes changed along with his scent. I assisted him through his shift yesterday during the blizzard. He's a strong lynx, like his father."

"You're his teacher?" Jean Phillippe asked.

Ben nodded. "His mythology class."

"I'm studying to become an art historian and restoration specialist," Derick said.

"Really? That's wonderful. There is plenty for you to restore amongst all the clan heritage homes. Perhaps something to bring you up to Canada," Jean Phillippe said.

"I'm not at that point yet, still need to finish my degrees and internship," Derick said. "Though, I would like to see the collections."

"I've been speaking with your mom. Did she perhaps...mention the holidays?"

"About traveling to see you. Yes, she mentioned it." Derick glanced at Ben and back to Jean Phillippe. "Does she know about you? Me? The... clan?"

"I've begun to explain things after she sent me a picture of you and how much you resemble me. With your appearance, I realized you would have inherited the genes to shift. It's why I sent you the journal when we couldn't talk." Jean Phillippe shook his head. "She doesn't understand everything, but I hope to reveal more to her during the holiday."

"She might freak out, but I don't know," Derick said.

"We'll take care of her. Help her understand. I promise we'll do this together, for her," Jean Phillippe said.

"Then I'll tell her to make travel arrangements to see you."

"This is fabulous. I'll contact her to help her with them. No reason she should pay for everything." Jean Phillippe smiled. "We'll prepare the first shift ritual to include you. There were four other new kits this winter season. We like to hold the ritual around the holidays for all the families to enjoy and celebrate their kits."

"That sounds wonderful," Derick said.

The phone beeped.

"That's our signal. I apologize, but until we get power back, this is the best we can do. I'll keep an eye on your kit," Ben said.

"Teach him well," Jean Phillippe said.

"It was good to see and speak with you. I'm sorry I didn't do it sooner," Derick said.

"It's all right, son, we'll make up for the lost time. Together."

"I like that. Bye... Dad."

Jean Phillippe smiled. His eyes watered a bit. "Bye for now, my son. I'll see you soon." He waved and disconnected the call.

Derick leaned back against the loveseat. He closed his eyes and let out a sigh while Ben took care of the laptop and phone.

"That was a wonderful conversation. A good start," Ben said.

"Now what?" Derick glanced over at him.

"Keep learning. Go to classes. Then every new moon, you place your paws in the snow."

Dreamy...Sensual...Forever Love

A quiet one, Nicole Dennis is the penname of an asexual author of different genres of fiction – both LGBT+ and hetero. Lots of characters, worlds, and stories build up in her head until she must get them down on the screen – anything from romance to fantasy to paranormal.

During the day, she works in a quiet office in Central Florida, where she makes her home, and enjoys the down time to slip into her imagination. She is owned by a feline companion – a fluffy house panther, known as Midnight the Void. A very special furbaby who is FIV+ and polydactyl on her front paws (fluffy danger mittens!).

Website: http://nicoledennis.net
Email: nicoledennis.author@gmail.com
Facebook:
Main: www.facebook.com/NicoleDennis.Author
Page: https://www.facebook.com/NicoleDennis.Musings/
Group: https://www.facebook.com/groups/nicoledennis.author/
Amazon: https://www.amazon.com/author/nicoledennis
Threads: https://www.threads.net/@ndennis_author
Mastodon: https://mastodon.lol/@nicoledennis
QueeRomance: https://www.queeromanceink.com/mbm-book-author/nicole-dennis/
Goodreads: http://www.goodreads.com/author/show/2791975.Nicole_Dennis

Current Books:

Pride Publishing
Southern Charm Series

1 – Rules of the Chef
2 – By the Numbers
3 – On the Green
4 – When in Bloom
5 – Following the Law
6 – According to Design
7 – Unexpected in the End (Coming 2025)
Freebies available on my website or email for PDF

Mischief Corner Books:
Secrets & Silk
Siren Publishing: (BookStrand.com)
Grant's Mechanic (MM)
Unholy Angel (MF Erotic Paranormal)
Fire Jaguars (MMF Paranormal)

1 – Fire Moon Dance
2 – Luna Moon Dance
3 – Dark Moon Dance
Other books are in the works

FatCat Books Ink (Self-Pub home):
New Stories:
Lyon Lynx Clan

Paws in the Snow (Prequel)

McShayne Bloodline

1 – McShayne's Dragon
2 – McShayne's Fae
3 – McShayne's Elf
4 – McShayne's Merman (Coming 2025)

Cheimon Tales

1 – Cracks in the Ice
2 – Strike's Stand (In the works)
3 – Mistletoe's Story (In the works)

Carnival of Mysteries (Multi-Author Collection)

1 – Dryad on Fire
2 – Flames of the Arcane

Re-Releases:
Walk Me Trilogy

1 – Walk Me Down the Middle
2 – Walk Me Through the Haze
3 – Walk Me Through the Darkness

7 Days of Christmas
Built Piece by Piece
At the Masquerade

* 9 7 9 8 2 2 4 0 9 5 4 1 4 *